The Little White Light

by Judy Ann Lowe

Illustrations

by Ayuna Collins & David Edward Martin

J.S. Pathways
Dallas, Texas

Illustrations by Ayuna Collins and David Edward Martin

Design by Carolyn Oakley, Luminous Moon Design

Published by J.S. Pathways, www.jspathways.com

Printed in the United States

ISBN-13: 978-1492168355
ISBN-10: 1492168351

To my loving Sam and my **_Little White Light_**,

both of whom I feel were sent into my life

when I needed them the most.

Penny was still awake and hadn't yet gone

to sleep when a little blink of a white light

appeared near the corner of the ceiling.

She had never seen it before.

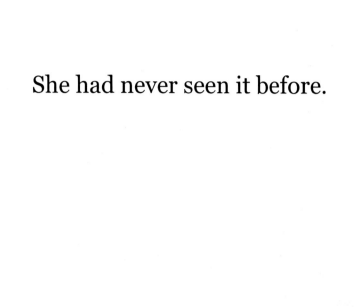

It blinked once very quickly then it stopped.

She thought maybe that it was a car light outside...

...but there was no car.

Then it blinked again.

Penny wasn't sure what that meant

or if she should even be afraid, but she wasn't.

Soon, she fell asleep and didn't think about the little light.

For the next several days and nights she didn't think about the little light or see it. Then it appeared again as if it had been on a trip and returned.

From then on, it was there every night

and in the early morning hours, also.

Sometimes, Penny even noticed it during the day.

When Penny was doing her homework one day,

out of the corner of her eye she saw it

streaming near her side.

Then it left.

Another time, she was helping her Mom wash the dishes and looked through the doorway into a dark bedroom. The little light streamed into the darkness just as if it wanted her to know it was nearby or that it was time for her to go to bed.

Penny smiled at that thought!

Sometimes it was large.

Sometimes it was small.

Sometimes it was round or rectangular.

It had appeared in the *middle* of a wall and it had streamed *across* the wall very quickly.

But most of the time,

it was in it's special place

near the corner of the ceiling.

Soon, Penny began to talk to the little white light.

She called it *her* "Little White Light."

Every night after she laid down and turned out her

bedside lamp, she greeted the little light by saying,

"Hello, Little Light. Hello, my Little Light.

Hello, hello, hello."

After a few seconds,

she repeated that greeting again.

Then, it would blink as if to let her know that it was there and that everything was okay.

Penny told her little light that she liked its little,

white, glowing energy and that it was

so comforting to her.

She knew it was with her

and watching over her.

Penny felt very calm, at peace, comforted and safe knowing the Little White Light was with her.

Even while playing outside.

Even while doing her homework.

Even while she was asleep.

It was definitely *her* spiritual

Little White Light.

No matter what kind of day Penny had,

she knew the Little White Light would be with her.

She knew it would be with her forever.

What a special way to start
and end each day with the
Little White Light!

May *your* light shine bright.

Good night!

With great appreciation to:

Ayuna Collins and David Edward Martin for their artistic creativity;

Carolyn Oakley for her expertise with book layout and creative direction;

and Karen Gresham Nickell for her unending support,

ideas and motivation.

About the Author

Judy Lowe is a retired Gifted and Talented teacher in the Dallas Independent School District in Dallas, Texas. She holds a Bachelor's Degree in Music Education, a Masters Degree in Elementary Education and a Certificate in Gifted and Talented Education.

Judy currently serves on the Board of Directors of the North Texas Book Festival and is a member of the Dallas Museum of Art, Texas Retired Teachers Association, Dallas ISD TAG Educators Alumni, KERA and the Texas Association of Authors.

About the Illustrators

Ayuna Collins and David E. Martin live and work in Los Angeles, California. While both have independent art careers, they also work as a collaborative, multimedia illustration team. Their differing backgrounds operates as a key component in their creation process. The team often works on several pieces at once, trading back and forth, each adding the next layer or element until the picture has come to life.

Ayuna Collins earned her undergraduate in dance and animation at CalArts. Her masters focuses on where a lack of memory and the artistic practice meet.

David Edward Martin is an artist and educator. Trained in filmmaking and motion graphics, he seeks out the nuanced connections between various modes of expression.

Enjoy these other award-winning titles by Judy Ann Lowe!

Available at Amazon.com, BarnesandNoble.com, indielector.store and from the publisher at JSPathways.com

Learn more about Judy's books, see a schedule of her upcoming events, and enjoy videos and photos at JSPathways.com and Facebook.com/JSPathways

Made in the USA
Columbia, SC
20 April 2021